This *naughty* book belongs to

_____

For Polly and Sheila

First published in Great Britain in 2014 by Oxford University Press

ISBN 978-0-545-90671-5

12 11 10 9 8 7 6 5 4 3 2 1   15 16 17 18 19 20/0

Printed in the U.S.A.   08

This edition first printing, September 2015

This book just ate my dog!

Richard BYRNE

WALKIES!

LET'S GO!

SCHOLASTIC INC.

Bella was taking her dog for a stroll across the page when . . .

. . . something
very odd happened.

Bella's dog disappeared.

"Hello, Bella. What's up?" said Ben.

**Ben decided
to investigate.**

But Ben disappeared too.

Suddenly help zoomed in . . .

. . . then vanished.

Things were getting ridiculous.

I'll just have to sort this out myself, thought Bella.

But . . .

Sometime later,
a note appeared.

It read . . .

Dear reader,

It would be lovely if you could kindly HELP US!

Please turn this book on its side and SHAKE...

Bella
x

1. Turn book around

2. Shake

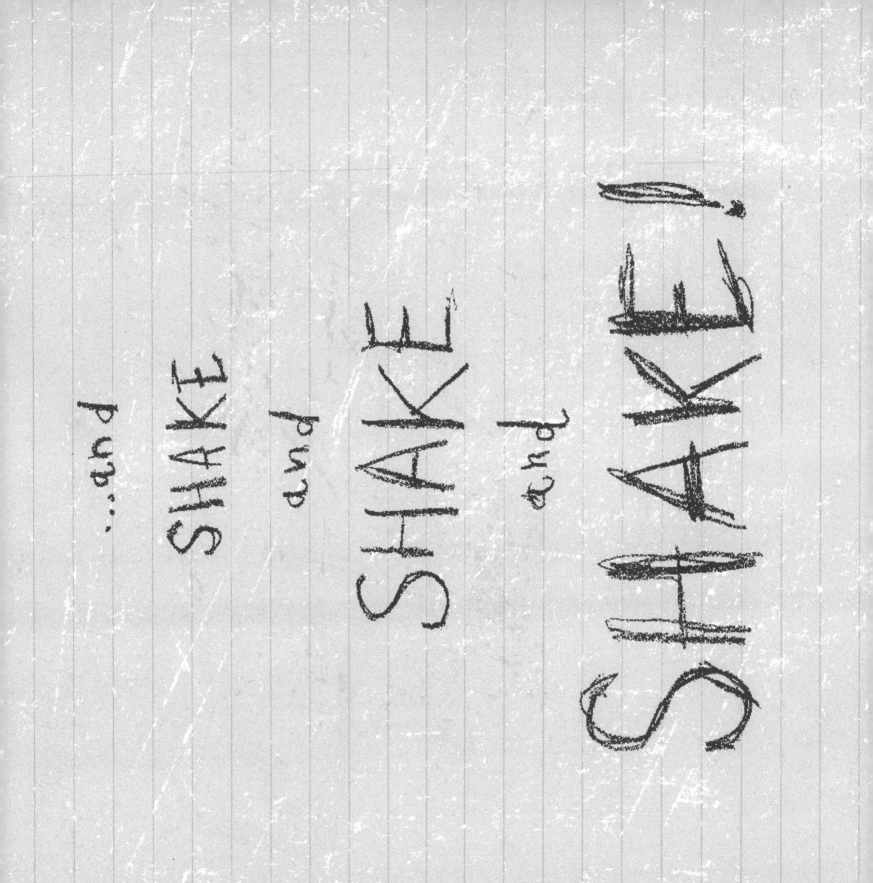

...and SHAKE and SHAKE and SHAKE!

...and one last little Wiggle.

Thank you.

Bella x

Everybody reappeared . . .

. . . and things got back to normal.

Well, almost!

Dear reader,
Please tell this book to promise
not to be so naughty next time
you read it.
Thank you.
Bella
x